B SMALL PUBLISHING

The Three Billy Goats Gruff

A puzzling version by
Steve and Sue Weatherill

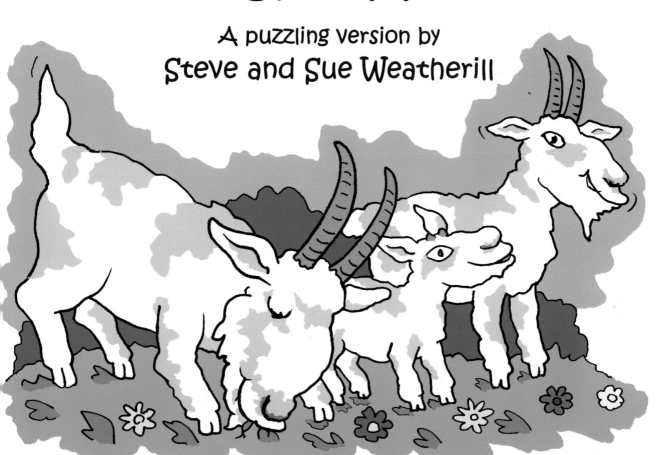

Finders Peepers!

Look carefully at all the pictures as you read the story. There are things to find and puzzles to do on every page.

We rabbits will keep popping up to show you what to do.

Three Nursery Rhyme characters are hiding in the story. Look carefully on each page and see if you can find them.

Humpty Dumpty

The cow who jumped over the moon

Ba Ba Black Sheep

Here is Nanny Goat Gruff. She wants to be in the story too. She appears in the pictures 3 times. Try and spot her.

The Three Billy Goats Gruff

Once upon a time there were three Billy Goats:

a little one

a middle-sized one

and

a great big one.

They all went by the name of Gruff.

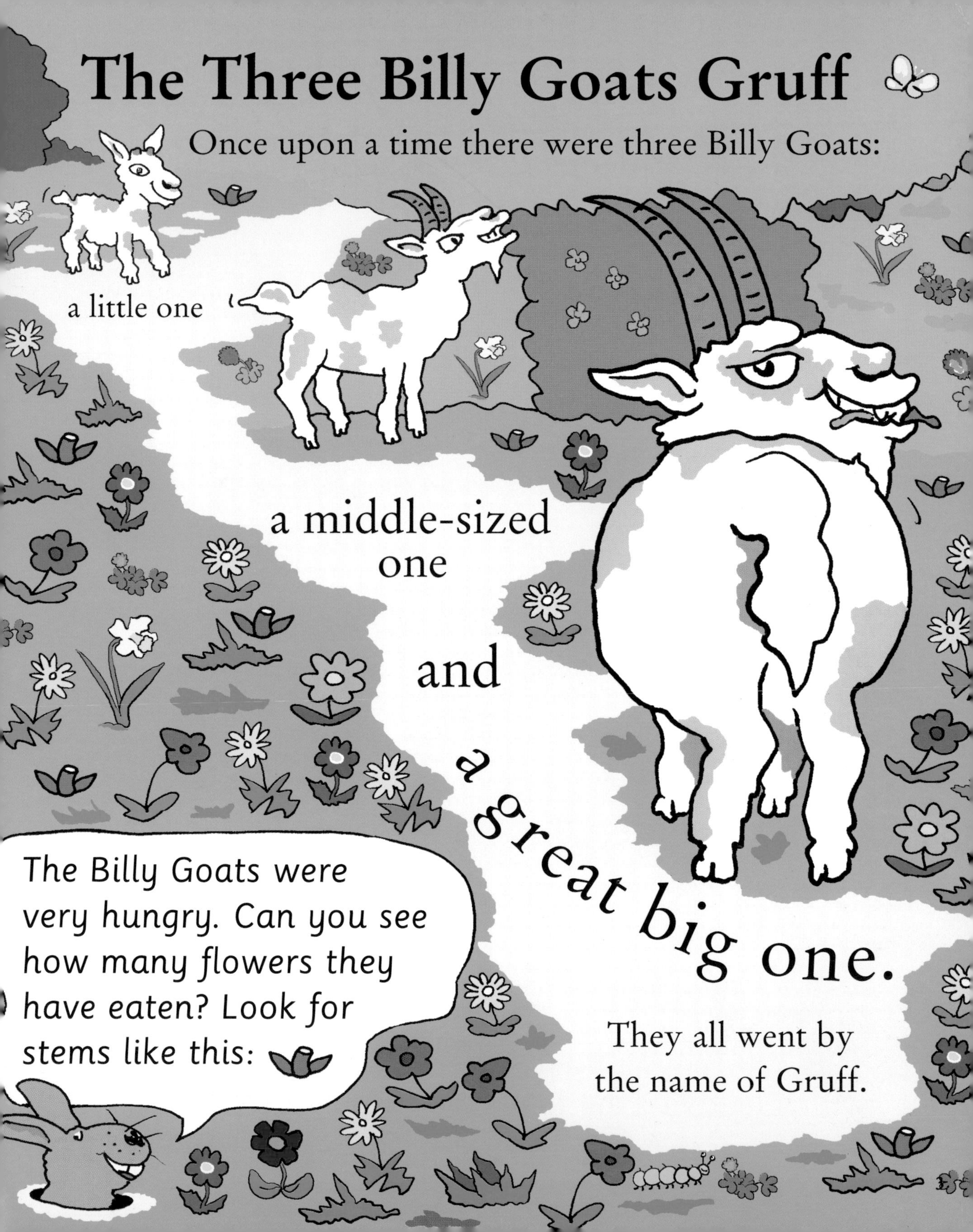
The Billy Goats were very hungry. Can you see how many flowers they have eaten? Look for stems like this:

They lived in a field by a river. On the other side of the river, the grass looked long and green. But to get there, they must cross an old stone bridge, and under that bridge lived an evil Troll.

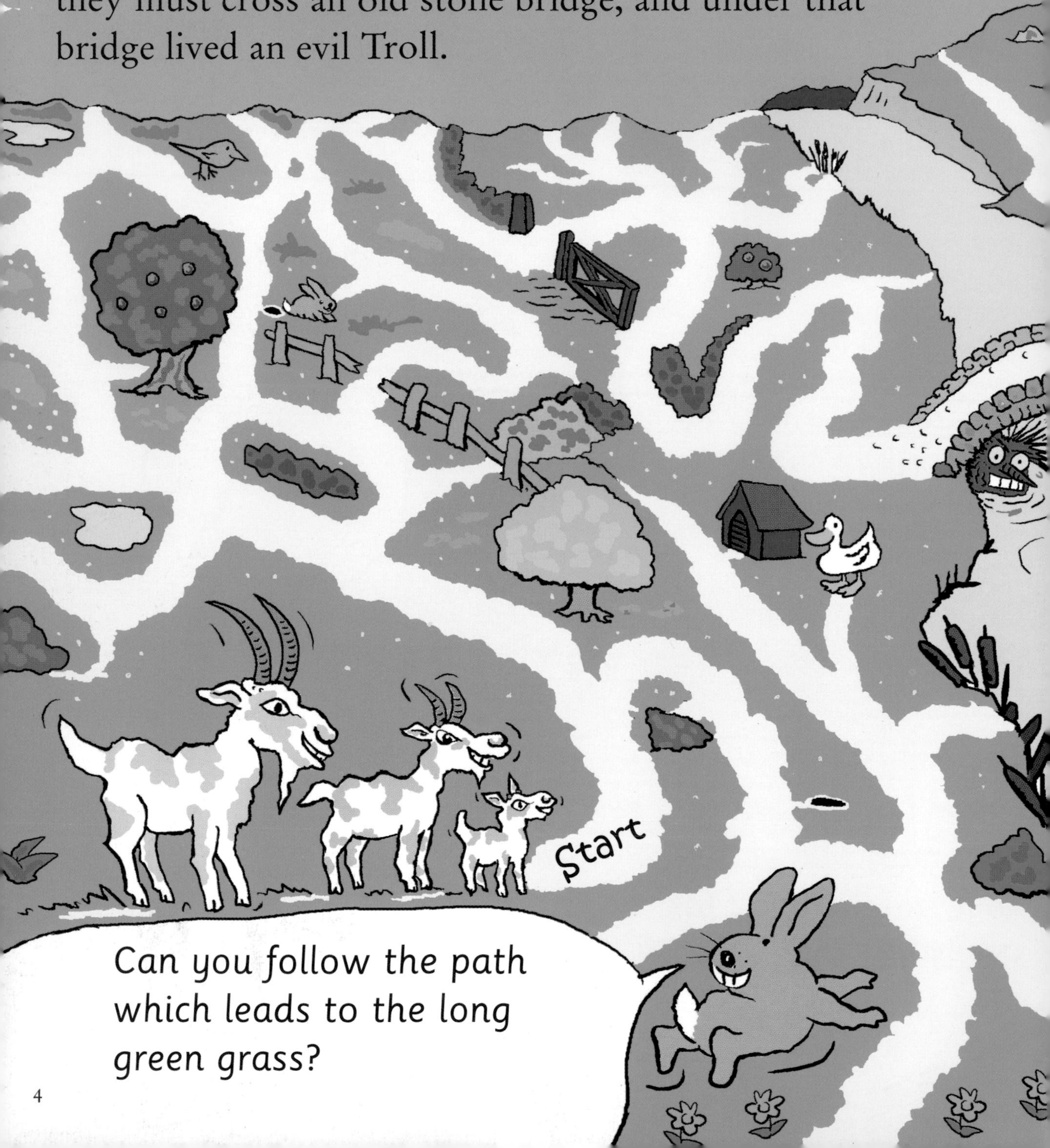
Start
Can you follow the path which leads to the long green grass?

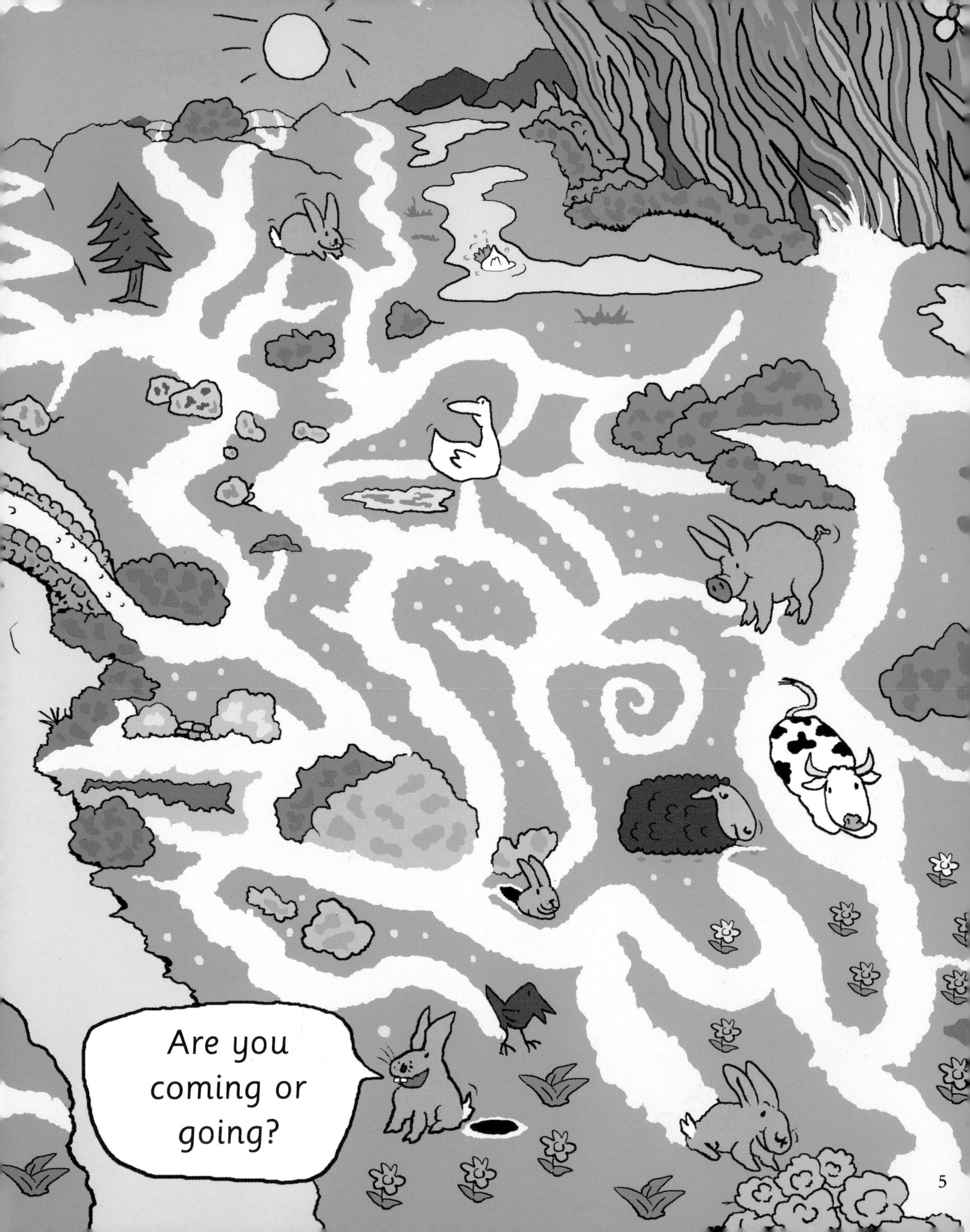
Are you coming or going?

The Troll was huge and hairy.
He had eyes like pies

and a

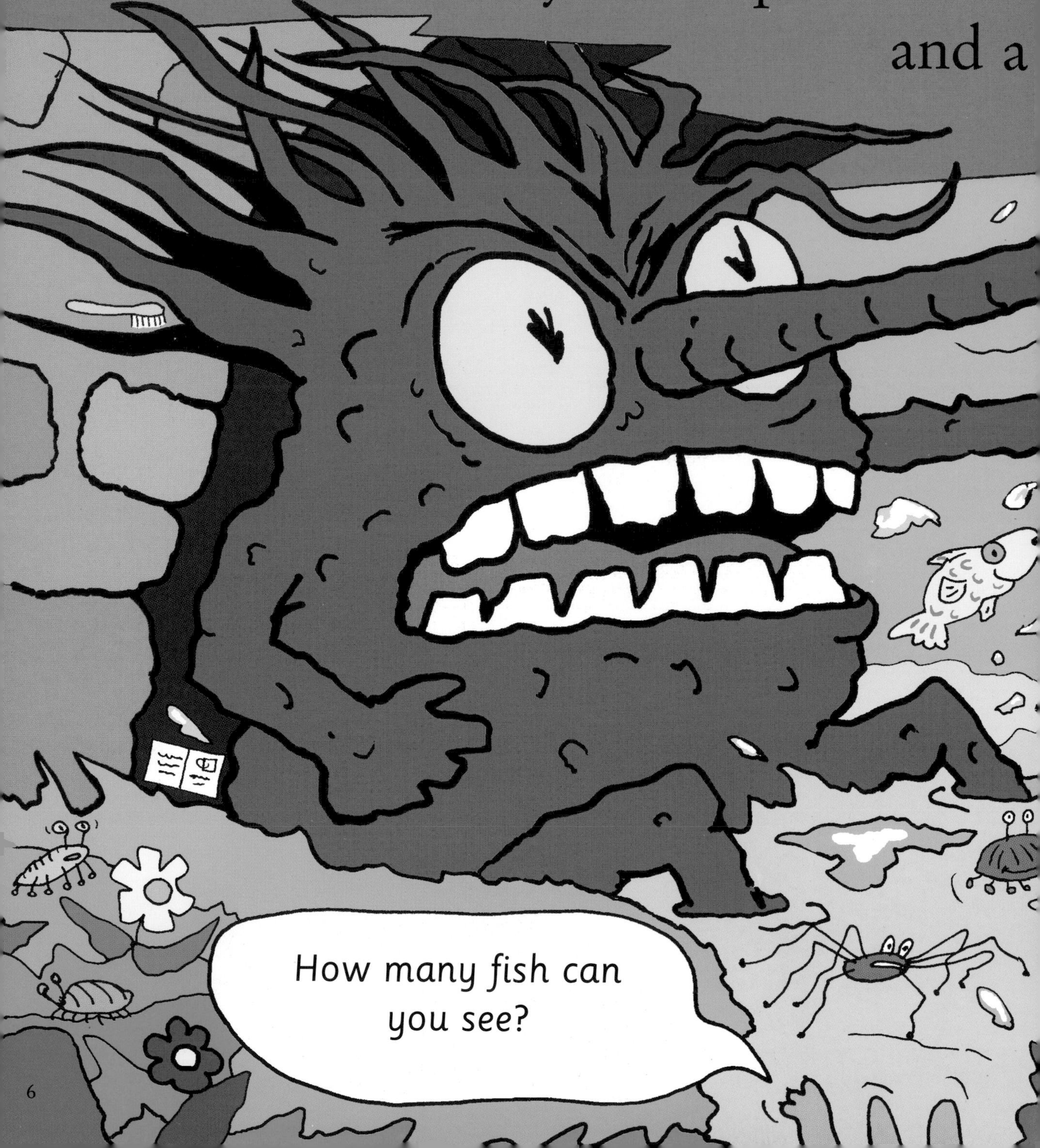
How many fish can you see?

nose as long as a pole.

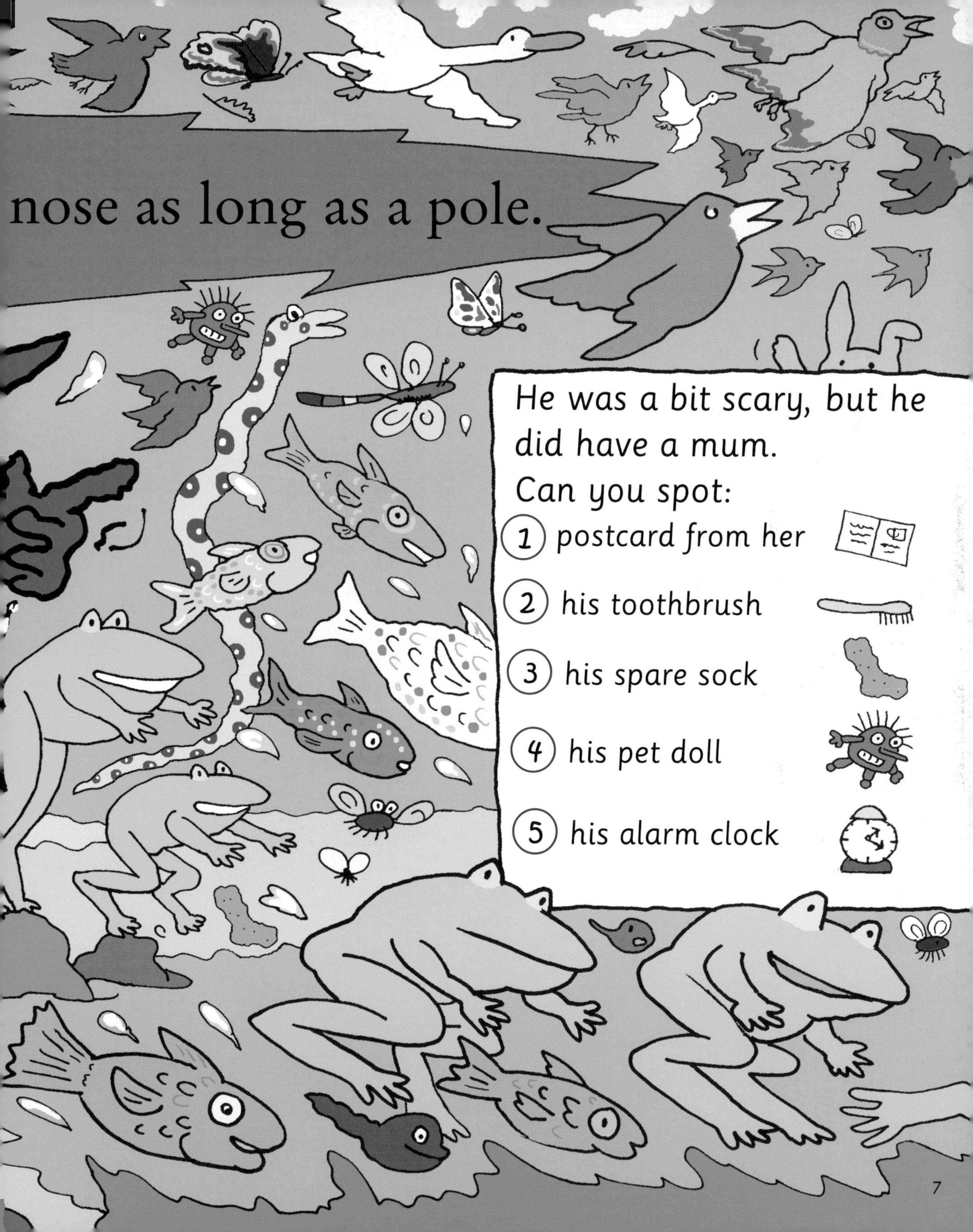

He was a bit scary, but he did have a mum.

Can you spot:

1. postcard from her
2. his toothbrush
3. his spare sock
4. his pet doll
5. his alarm clock

‘I’m going to cross the bridge and eat the long green grass,’ said the smallest Billy Goat Gruff. So he went trip-trapping over the bridge.

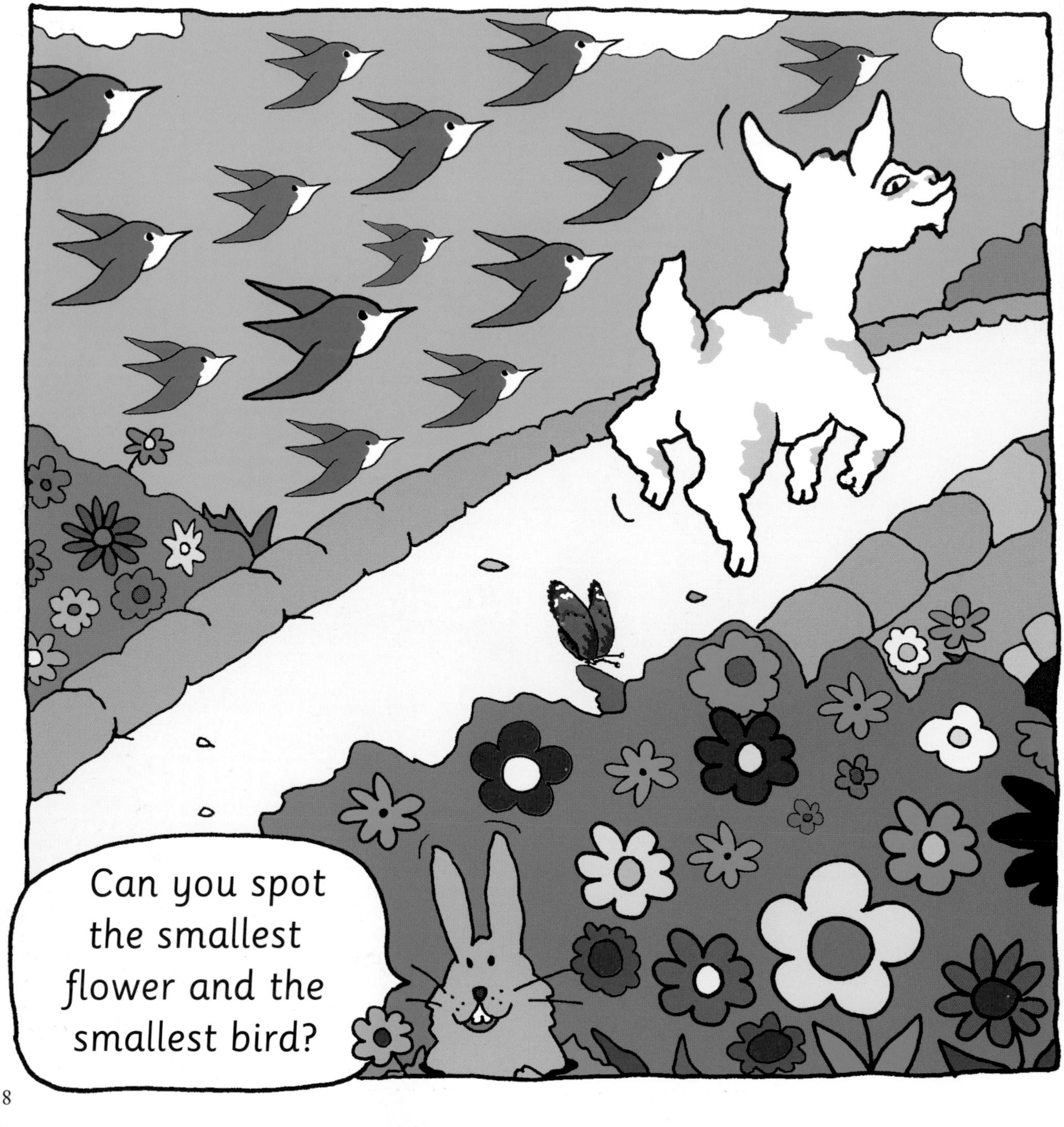
Can you spot the smallest flower and the smallest bird?

'Ho!' shouted the Troll. 'Who's that trip-trapping over MY bridge?'

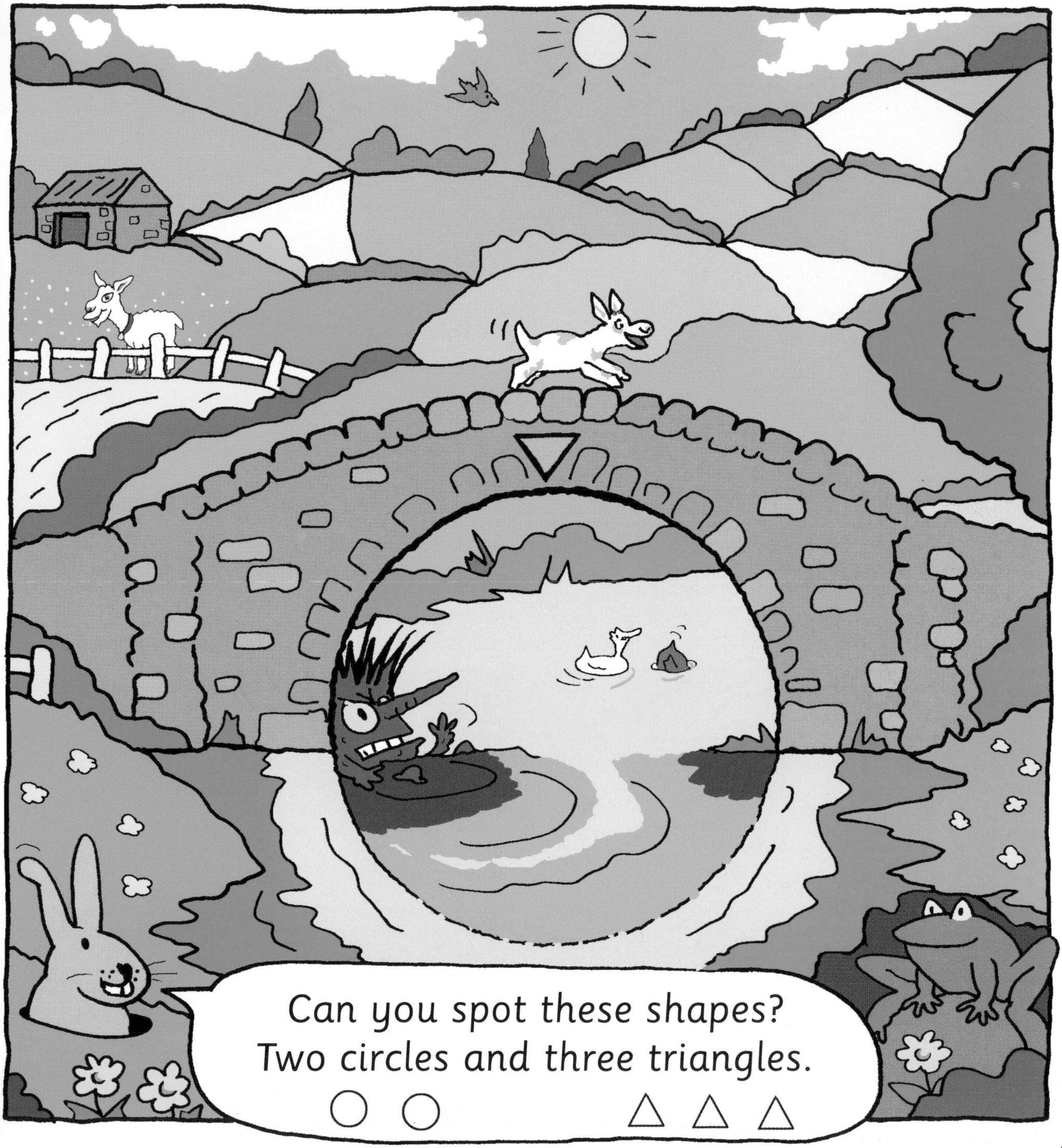
Can you spot these shapes?
Two circles and three triangles.

'It's only me,' said the teeny, tiniest Billy Goat Gruff in his teeny, tiny, squeaky, little voice. 'I'm going to eat the long grass and make myself fat.'

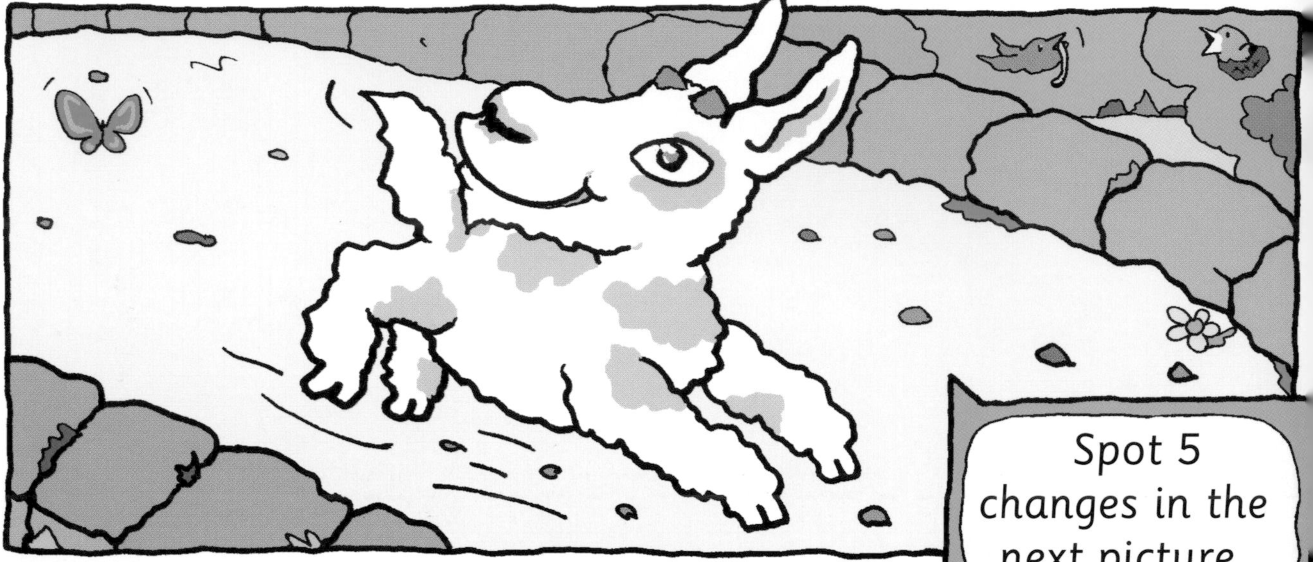
Spot 5 changes in the next picture.

'Well, I'm going to blobble and squobble and gobble you up!' shouted the Troll in his hairy, scary, don't-you-dare-me voice.

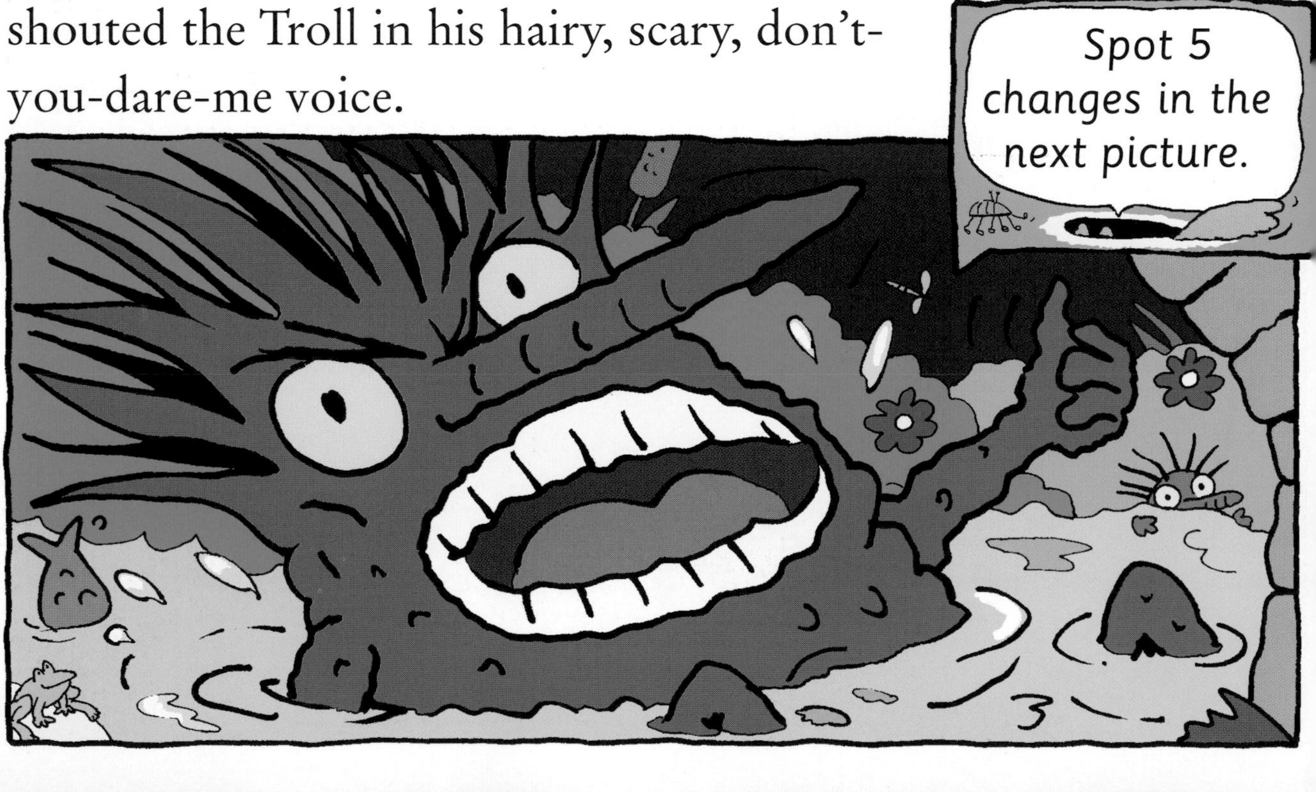
Spot 5 changes in the next picture.

'Oh no, please don't eat me,' said the teeny, tiny Billy Goat Gruff, in his teeny, tiny, squeaky, little voice. 'I'm really small. One mouthful and I'd be gone. Wait for the second Billy Goat Gruff. He is much bigger and tastier.'

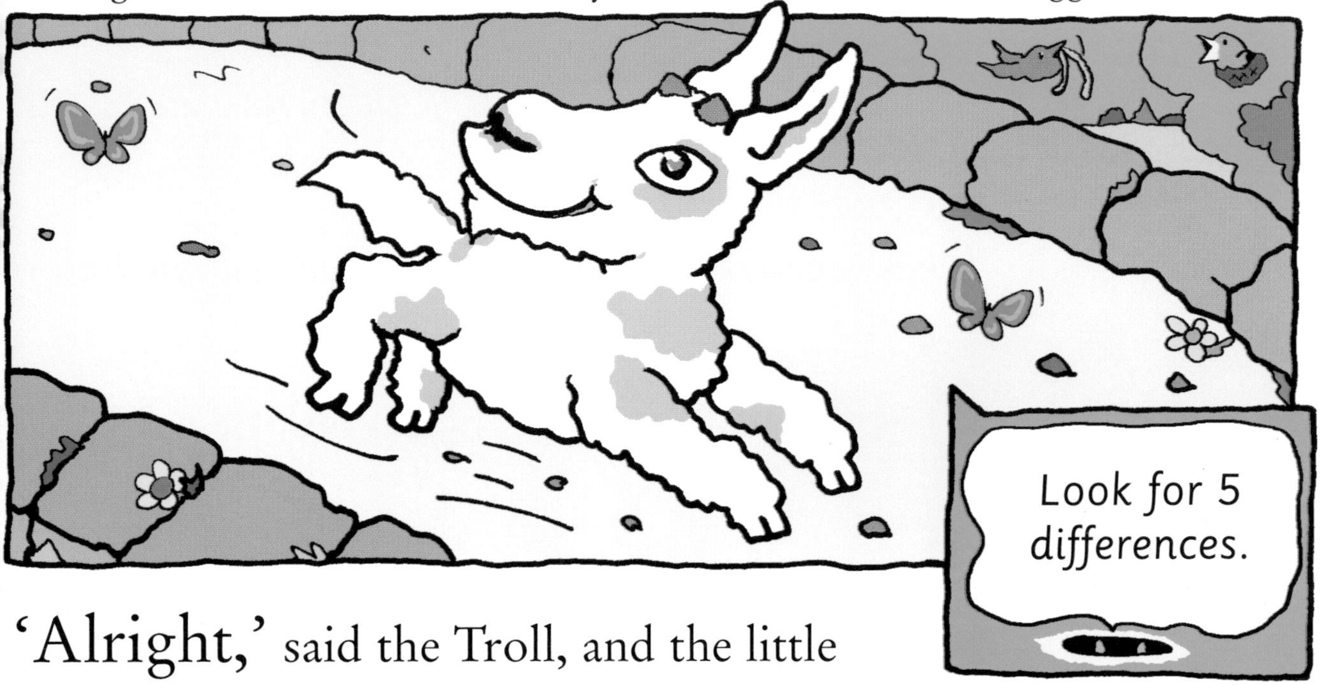
Look for 5 differences.

'Alright,' said the Troll, and the little Billy Goat Gruff scampered off across the bridge.

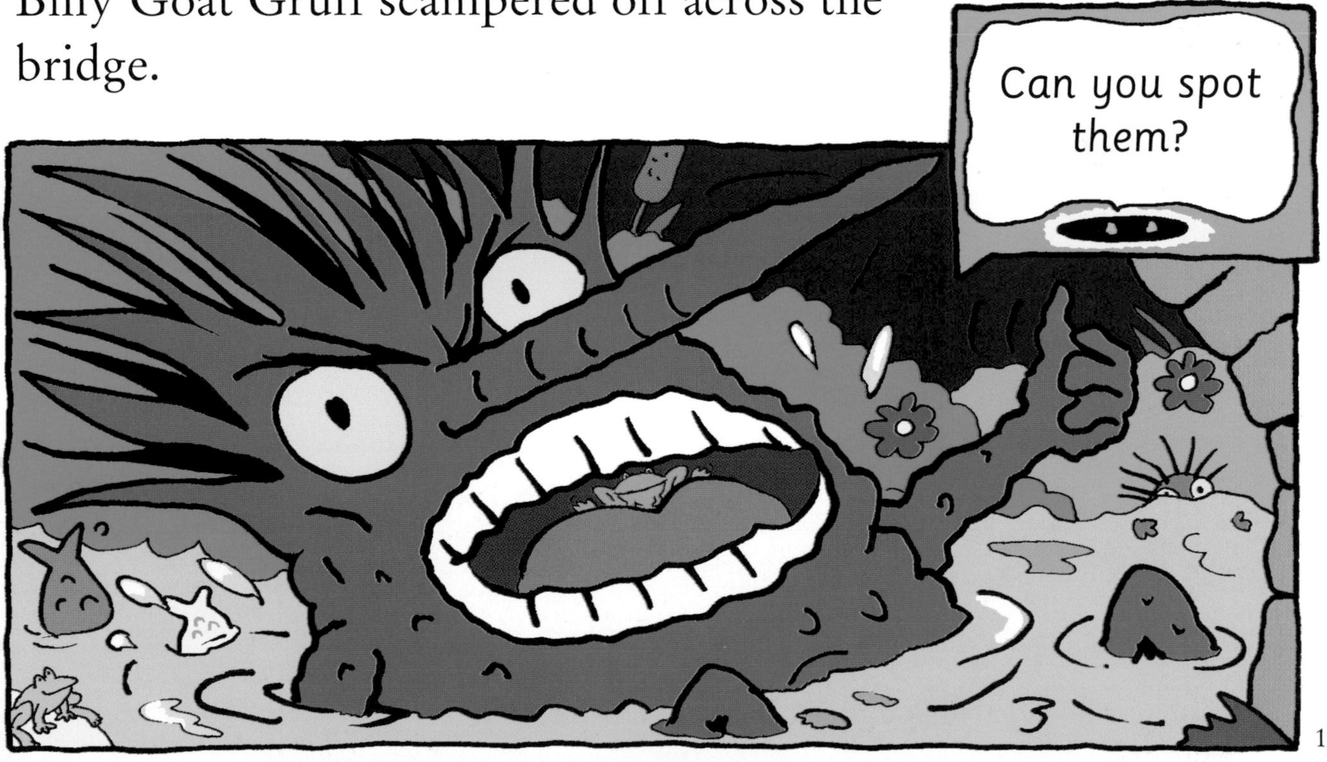
Can you spot them?

The Troll was just dozing off when he heard a louder trip-trap, trip-trap above his head.

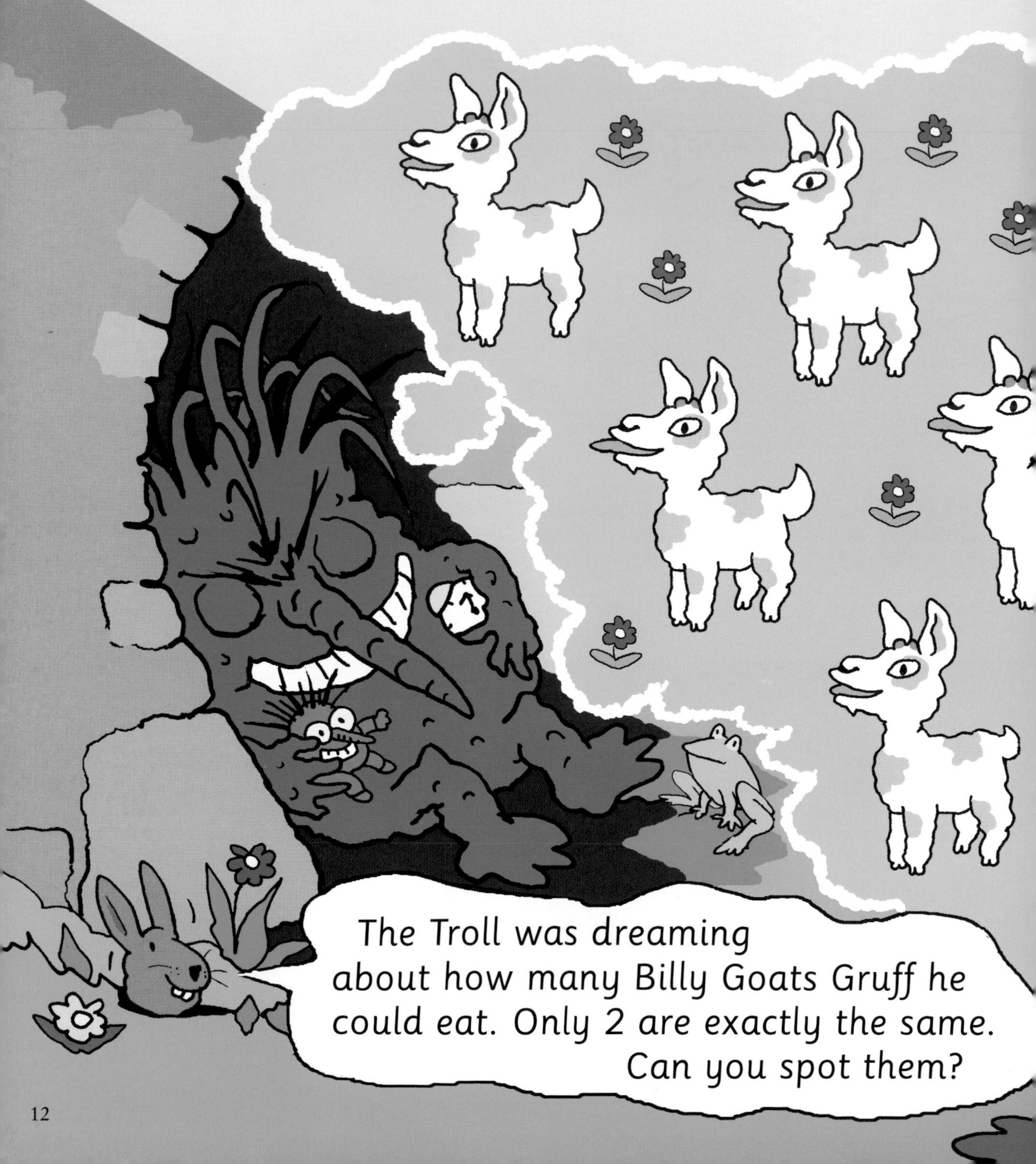
The Troll was dreaming about how many Billy Goats Gruff he could eat. Only 2 are exactly the same. Can you spot them?

‘Ho, Ho!’ shouted the Troll, ‘Who’s that trip-trapping over MY bridge?’

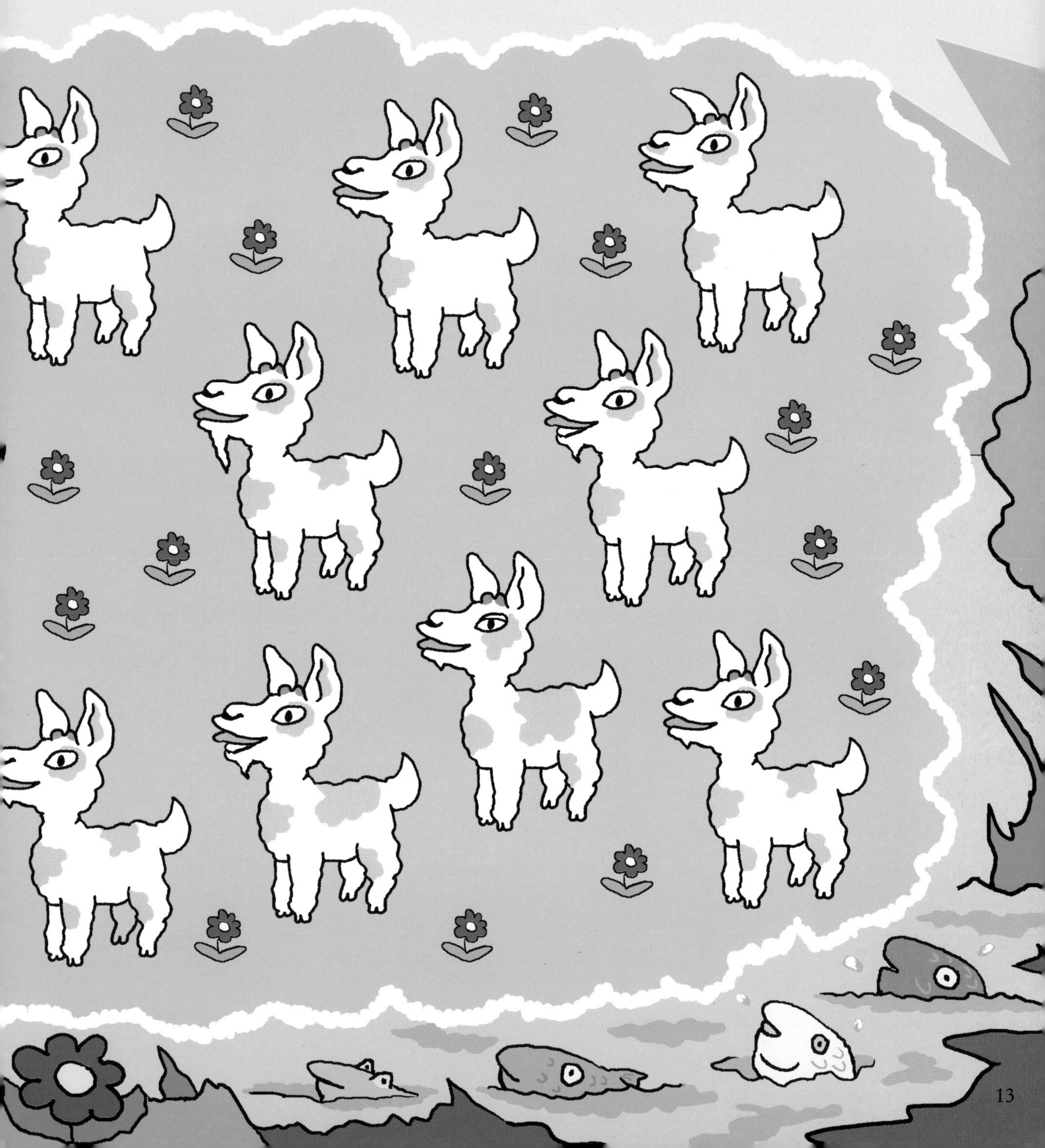

'It's only me,' said the second Billy Goat Gruff in a not-so-teeny, tiny voice. 'I'm going to eat the long grass and make myself fat.'

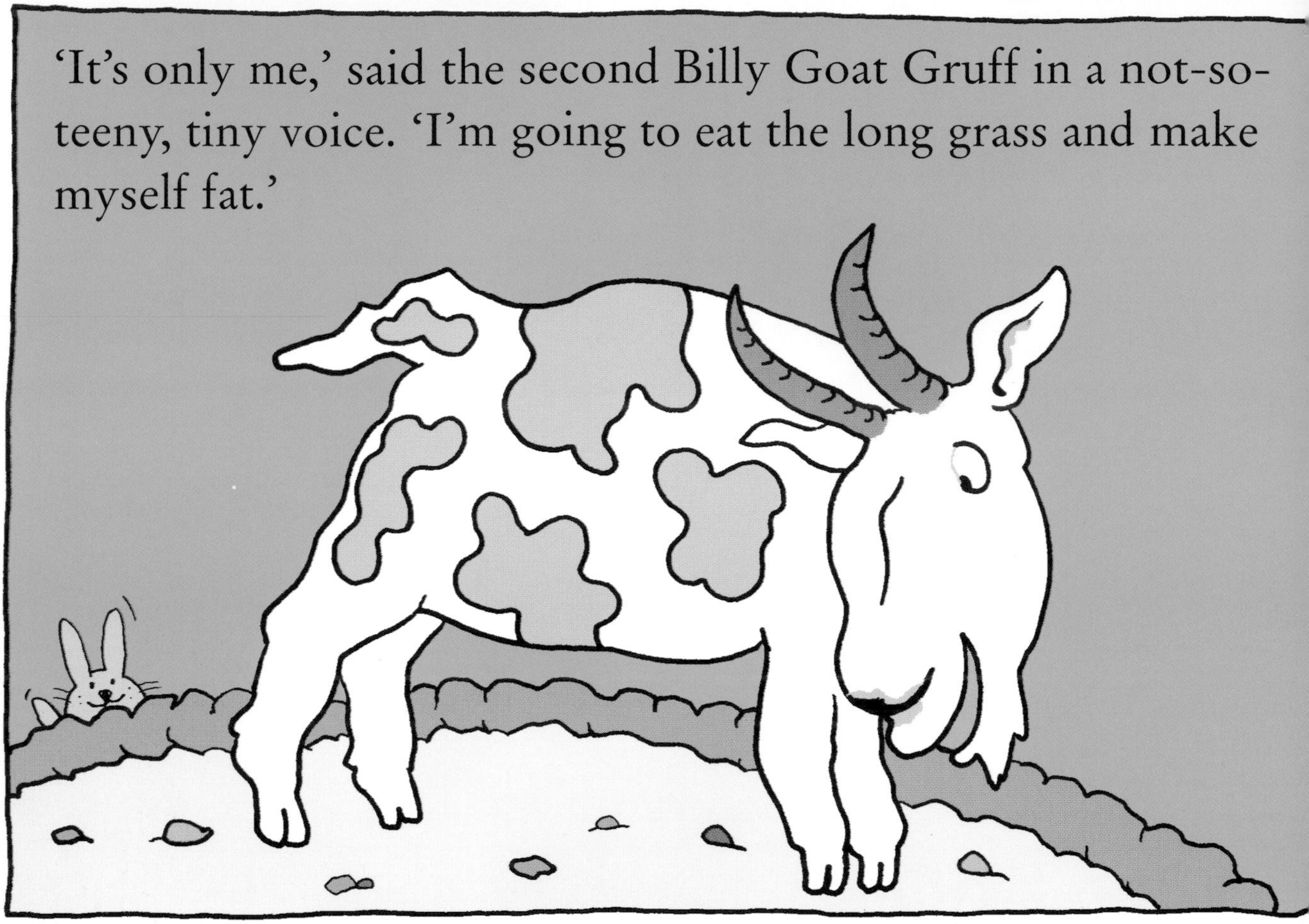

'Well, I'm going to flobble and drobble and gobble you up!' shouted the Troll in his hairy, scary don't-you-dare-me voice.

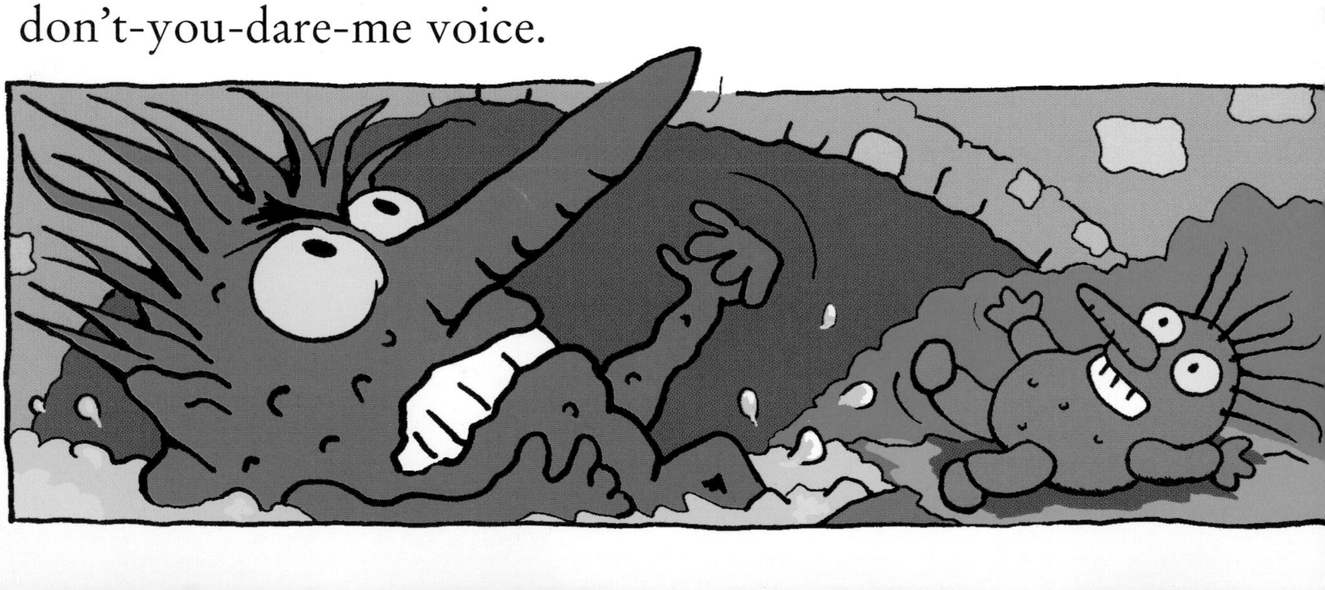

'Oh no, please don't eat me,' said the not-so-teeny, tiny Billy Goat Gruff. 'I'm bigger than the little Billy Goat Gruff, but the third Billy Goat Gruff is much bigger and tastier. Wait until he comes.'

'Alright,' said the Troll, and the second Billy Goat Gruff scampered off across the bridge.

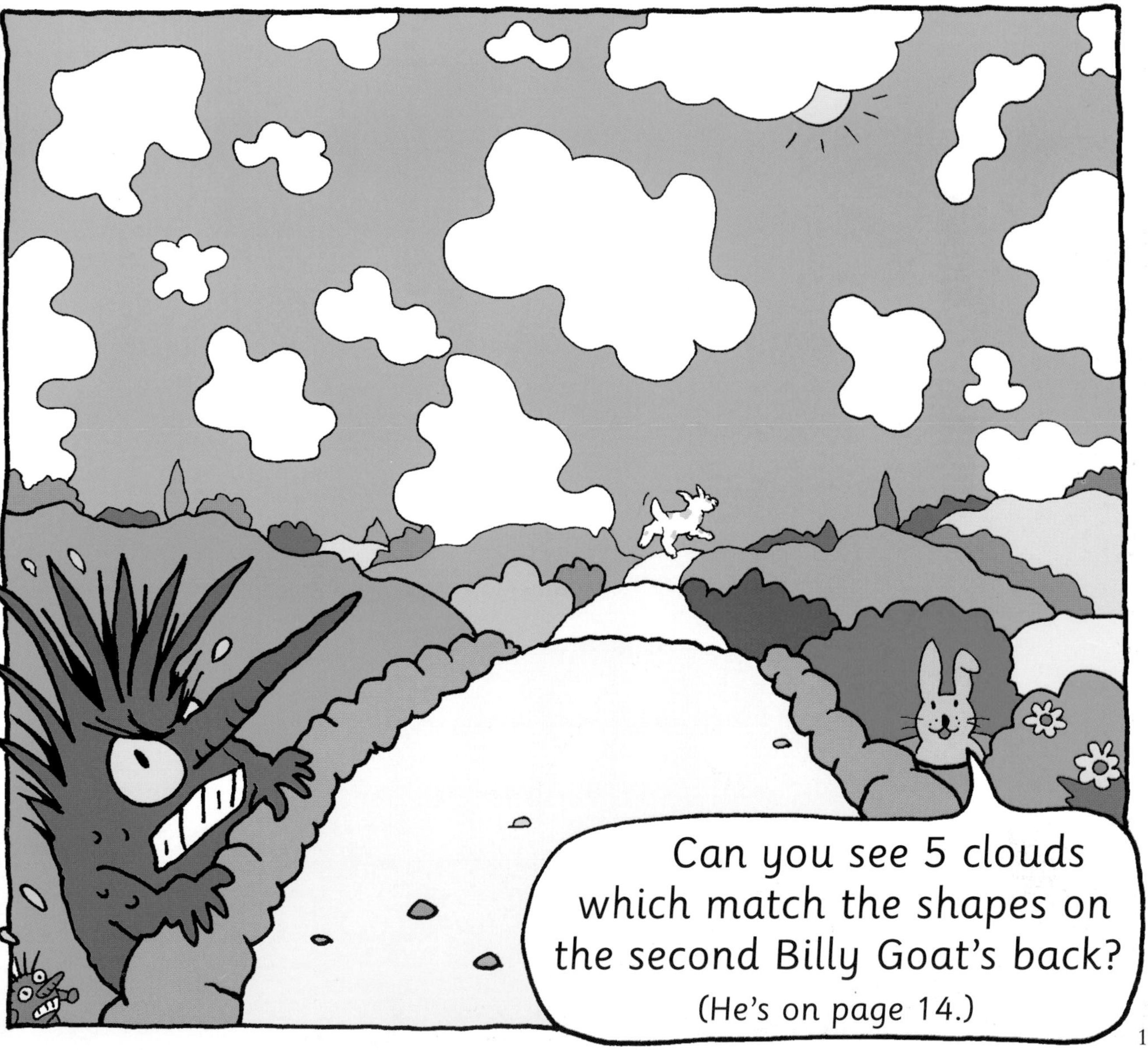
Can you see 5 clouds which match the shapes on the second Billy Goat's back?
(He's on page 14.)

The Troll was just dozing off again and started to dream. Suddenly he was woken by a very loud **trip-trap, trip-trap** above his head. The bridge began to creak and shake.

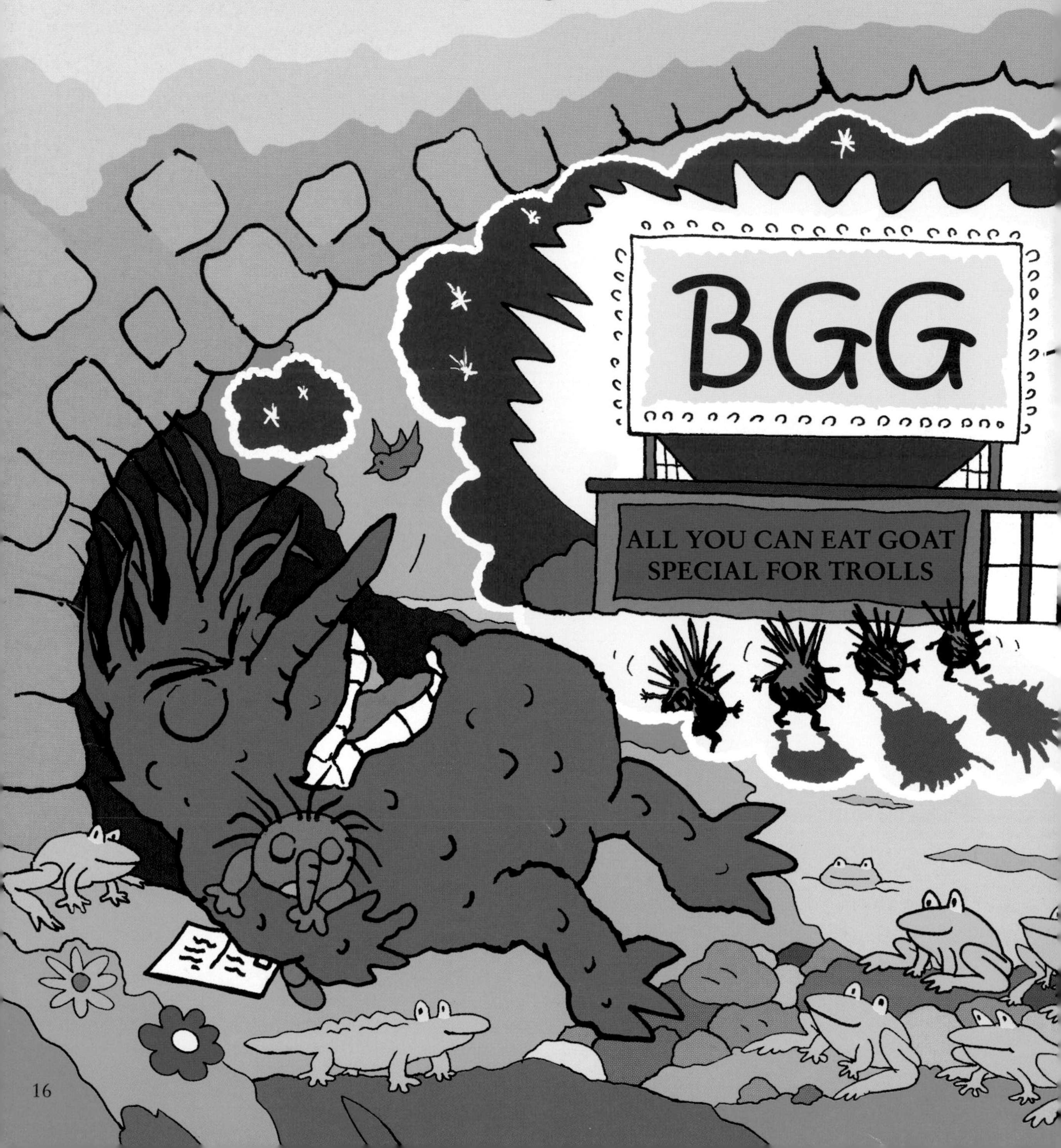
BGG
ALL YOU CAN EAT GOAT
SPECIAL FOR TROLLS

'Ho, Ho. Ho!' shouted the Troll. 'Who's that trip-trapping over MY bridge?'

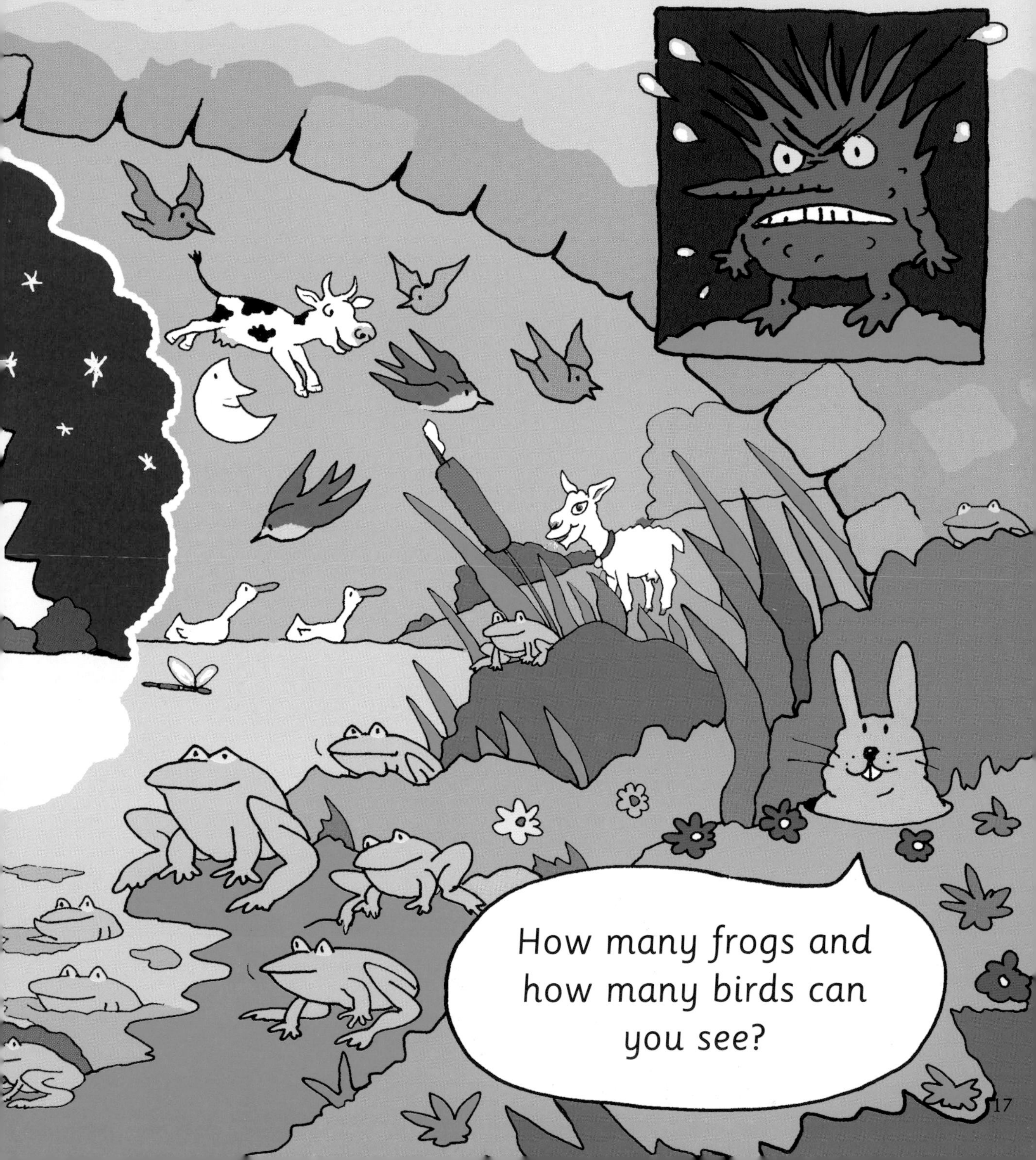
How many frogs and how many birds can you see?

'It is me, the big Billy Goat Gruff,' said the biggest Billy Goat in a voice even more hairy, scary, don't-you-dare-me than the Troll's.

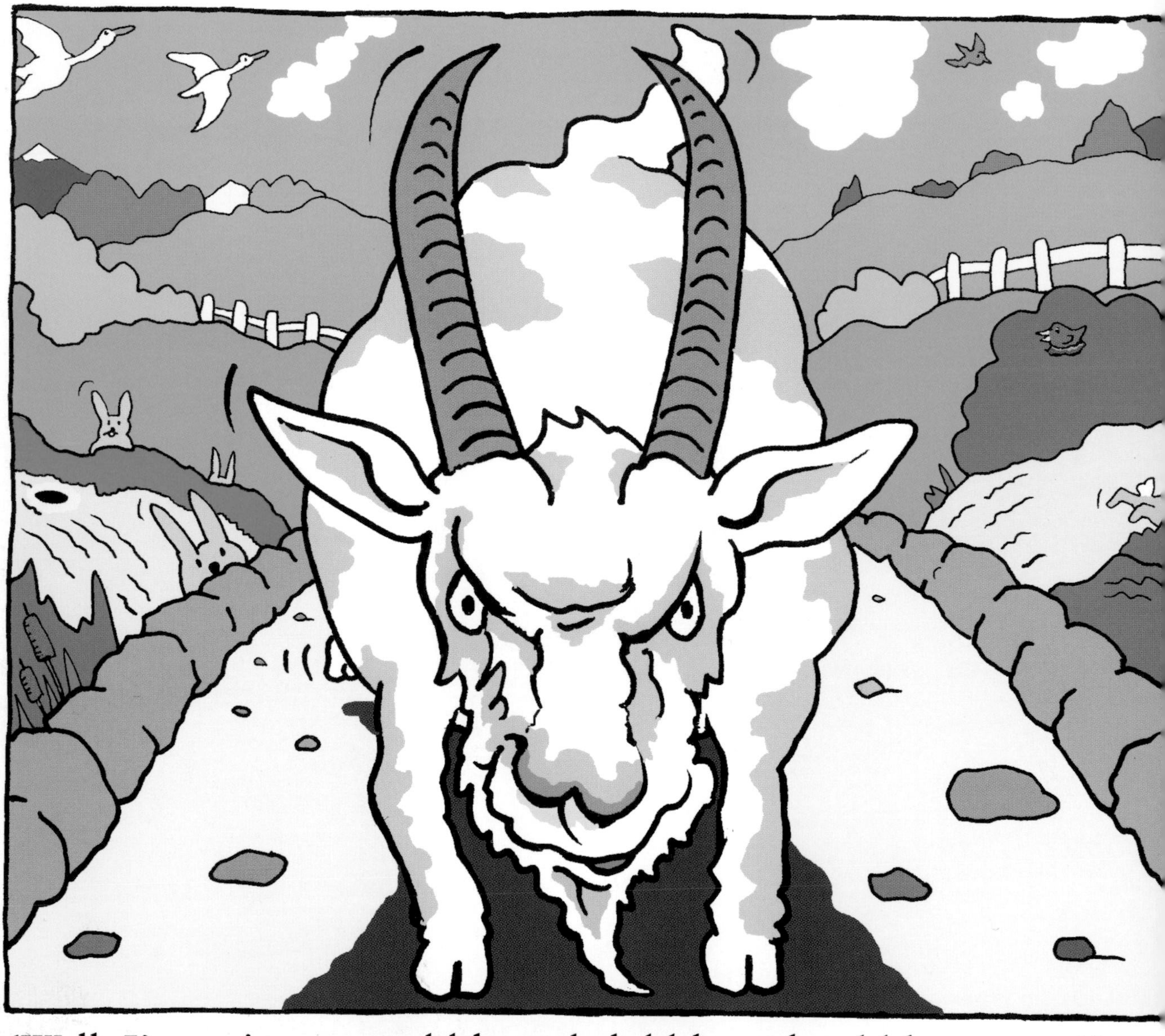

'Well, I'm going to probble and slobble and gobble you up!' shouted the Troll. He didn't sound so sure this time.

'Just you try,' replied the big Billy Goat Gruff. 'I've got two horns to poke out your eyes and four hooves to crush up your bones.'

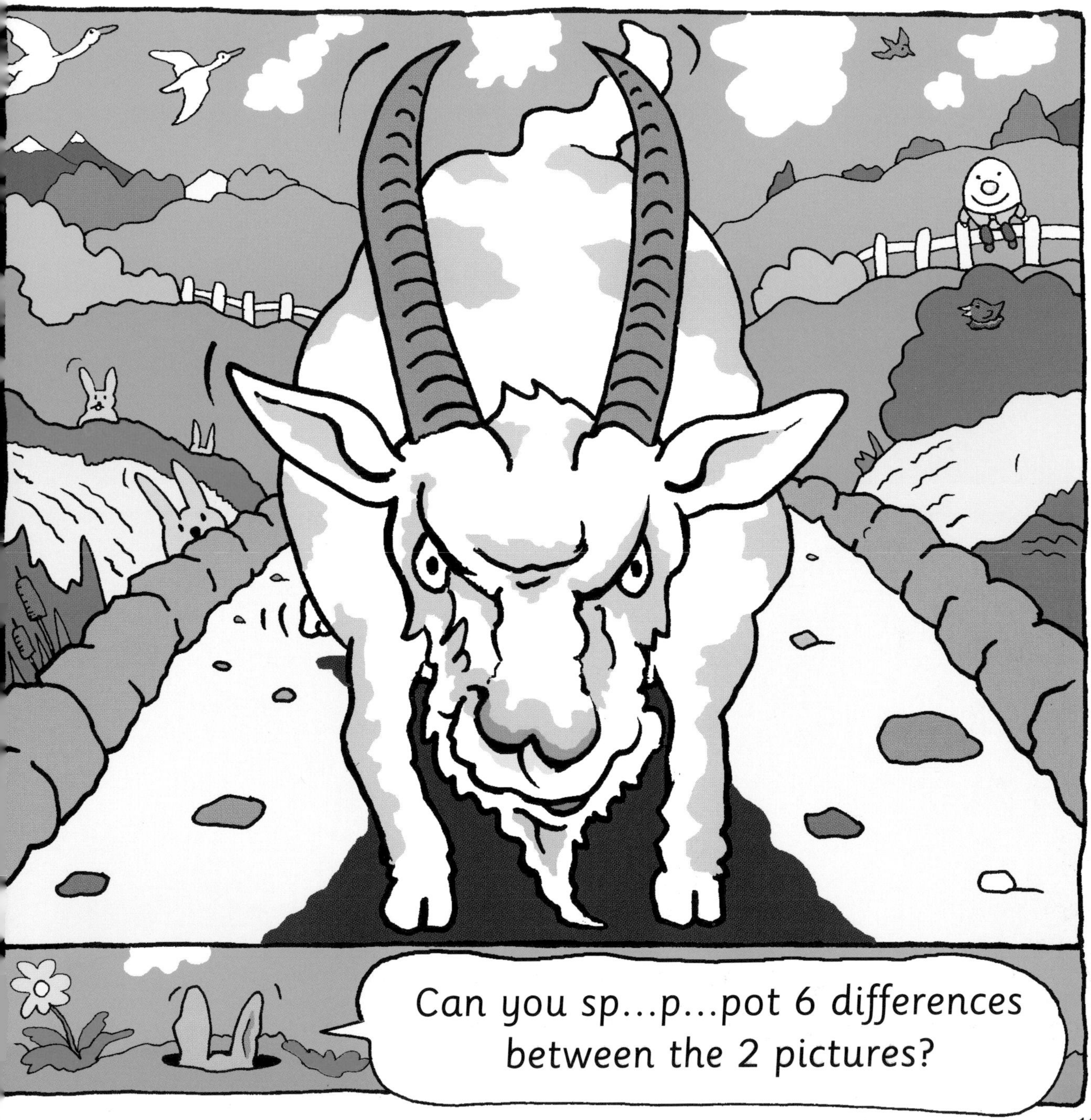
Can you sp...p...pot 6 differences between the 2 pictures?

The big Billy Goat Gruff rushed at the Troll. He crushed him with his hooves and tossed him into the river.

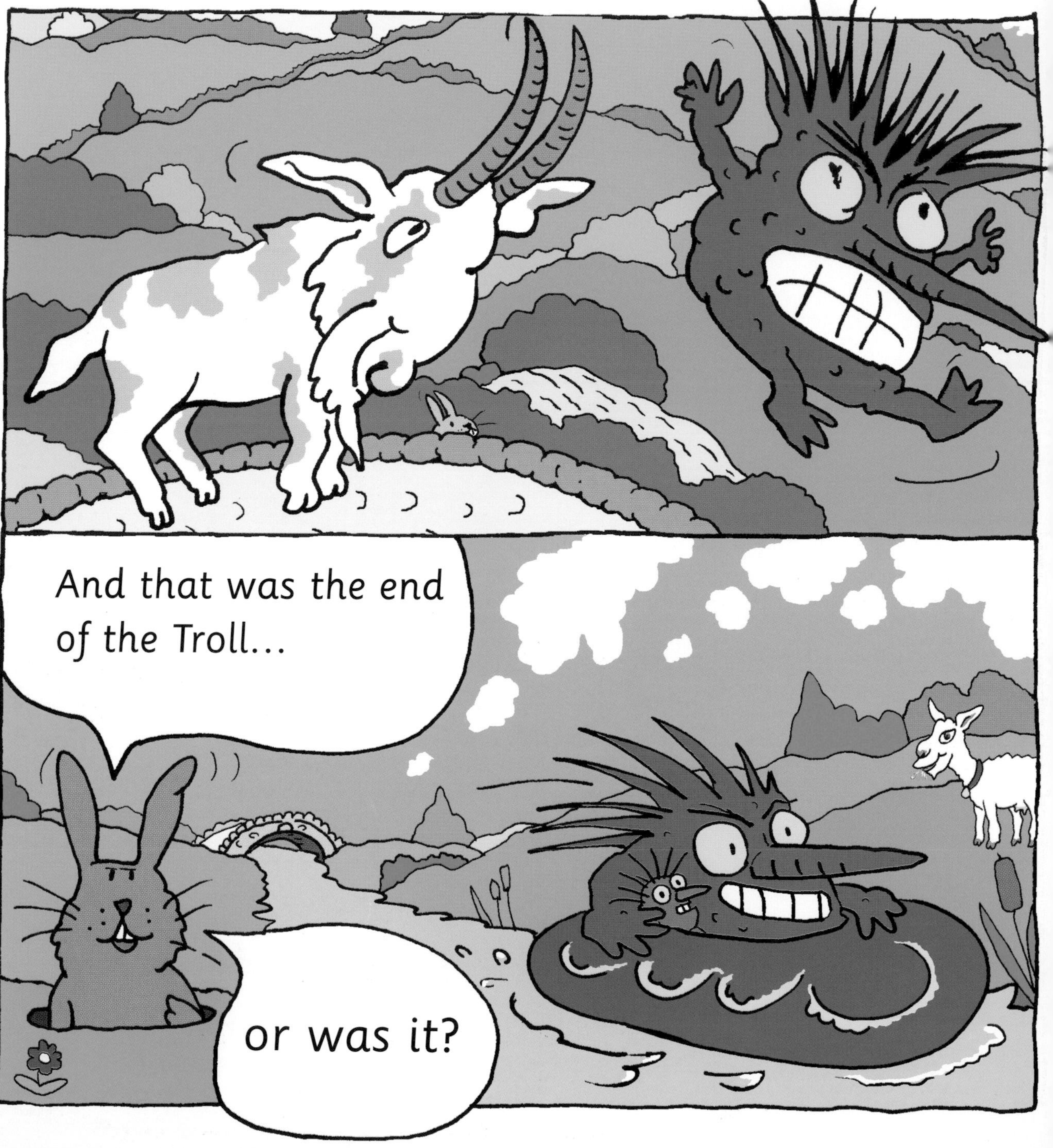
And that was the end of the Troll...
or was it?

Then he joined the two other Billy Goats who were eating the long, green grass. They ate and ate and grew fatter and fatter, so that when it was time to trip-trap home across the bridge, their legs could hardly carry them.

The end

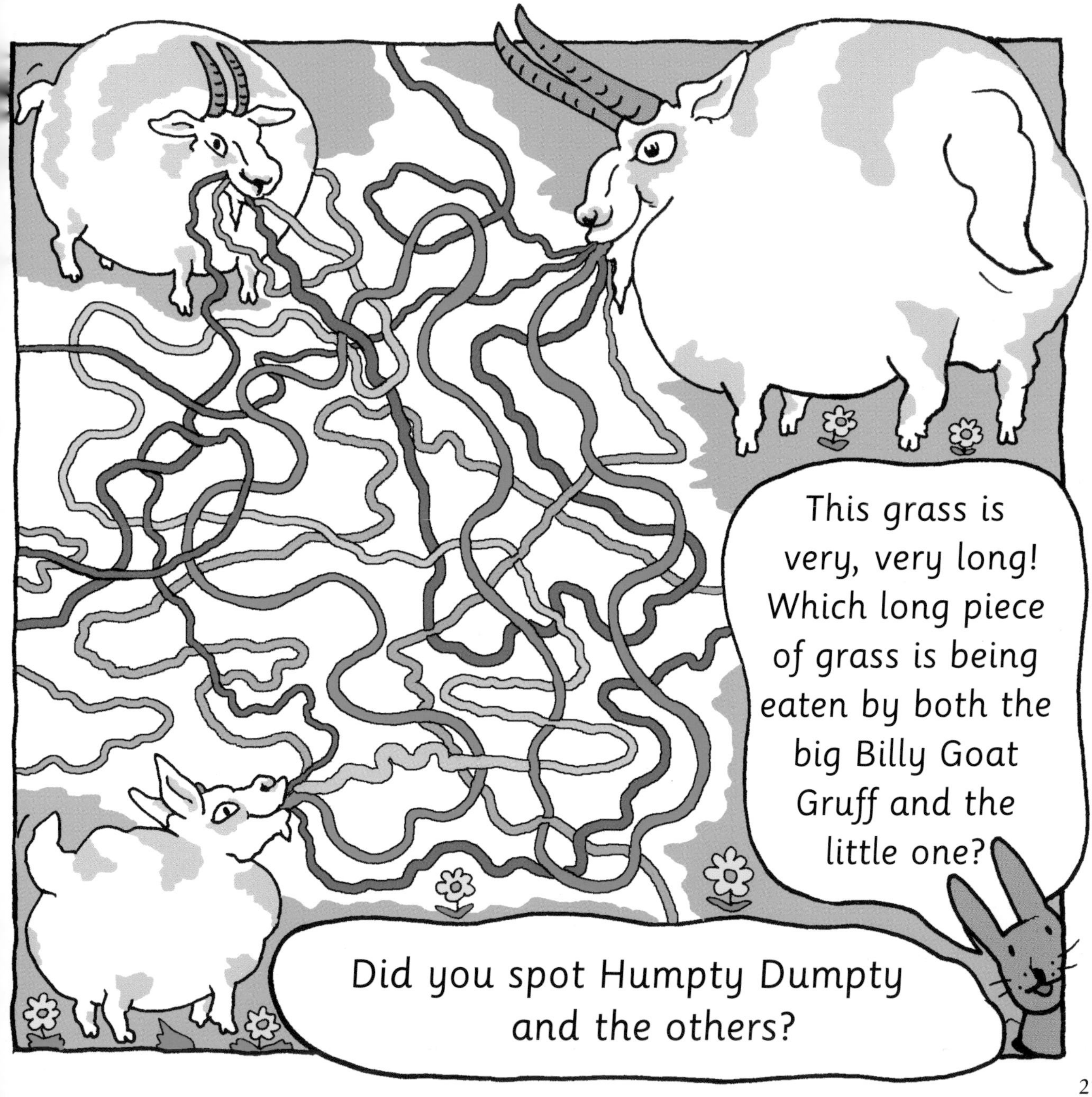
This grass is very, very long! Which long piece of grass is being eaten by both the big Billy Goat Gruff and the little one?
Did you spot Humpty Dumpty and the others?

Answers

Cover: 5 rabbits

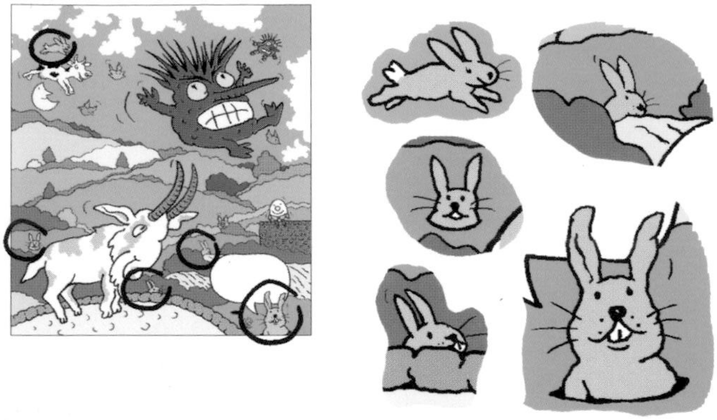

Page 3: 8 flower stems

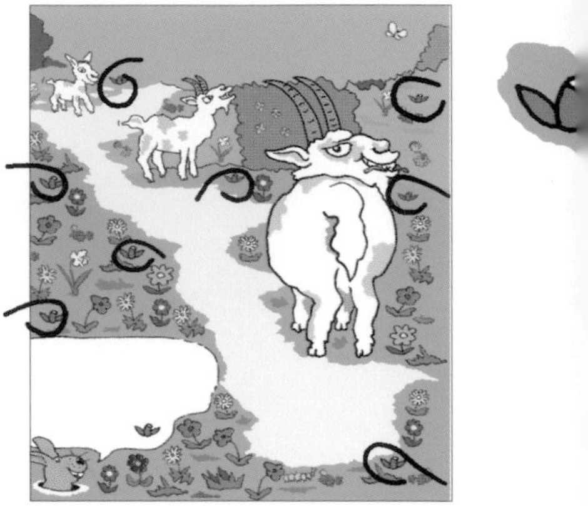

Pages 4, 5: maze

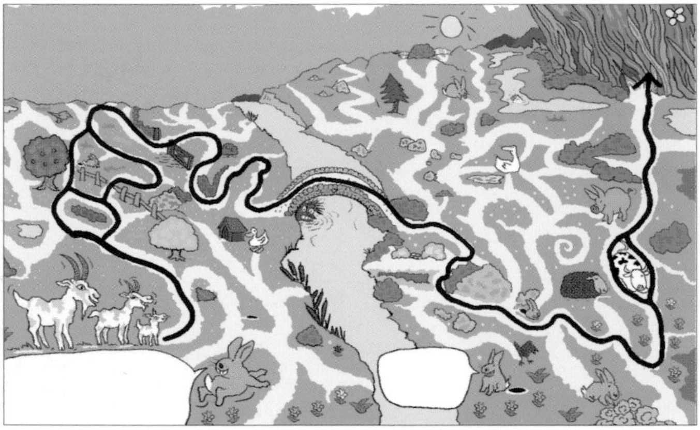

Pages 6, 7: Troll's things

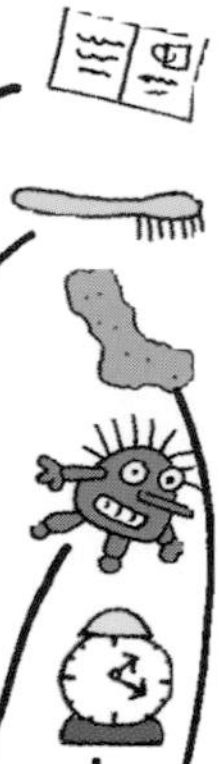

postcard

toothbrush

sock

toy

clock

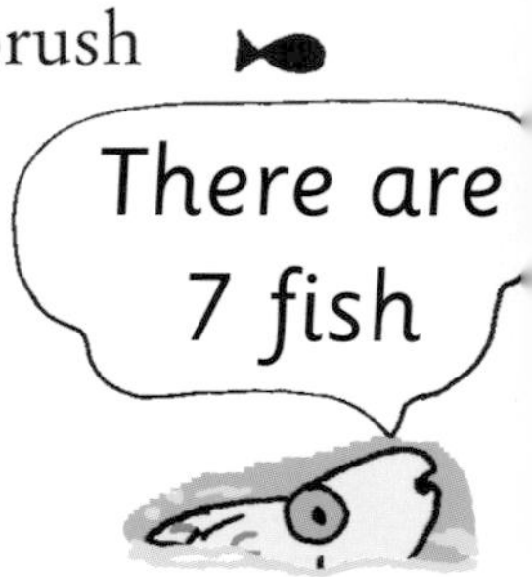
There are 7 fish

Pages 6, 7

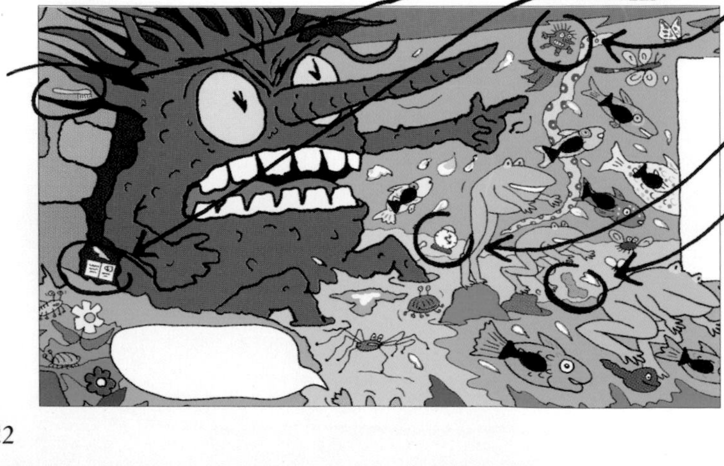

Page 8: smallest bird

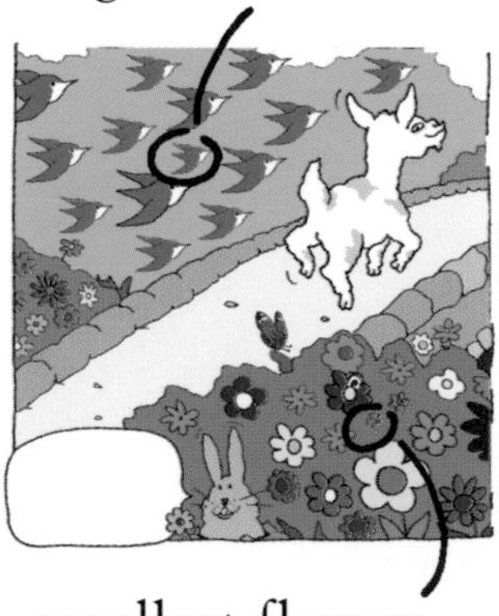

smallest flower

Page 9: shapes

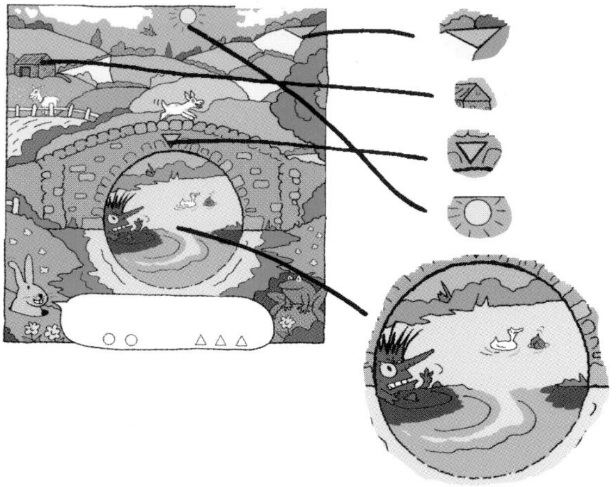

Pages 10, 11: spot the difference

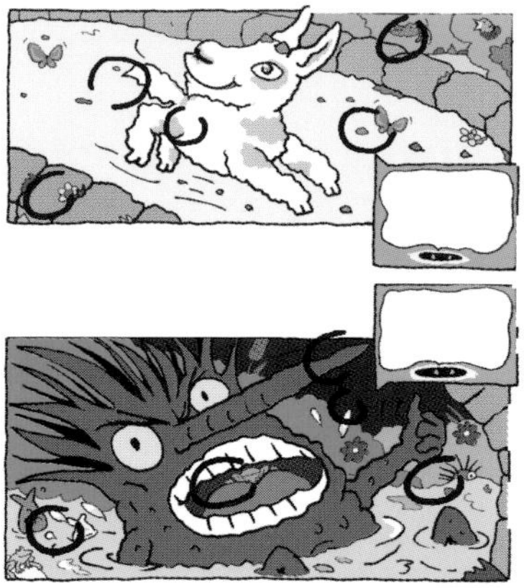

Page 11

1 two worms
2 missing patch
3 extra butterfly
4 flower
5 tail moved

1 longer nose
2 missing fly
3 frog in throat
4 extra fish
5 dolly in deeper water

Pages 12, 13: find 2 little Billy Goats the same.

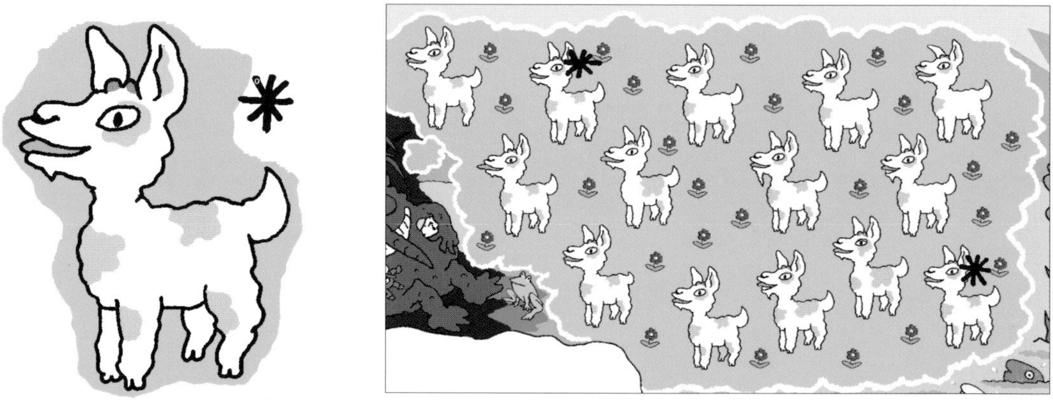

Pages 14,15: match 5 clouds to the shapes on the Billy Goat's back.

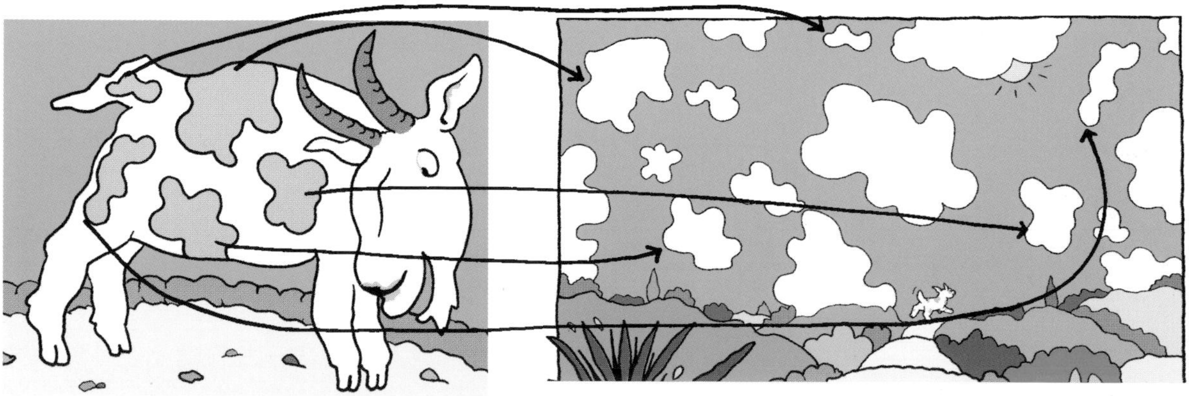

Pages 16, 17: counting

There are 15 frogs

And 8 birds

Including us!

Page 18, 19: spot the difference

Page 19

1 cloud
2 mountain
3 Humpty Dumpty
4 rabbit missing
5 white stone
6 missing rabbit hole

Page 21: long grass

Humpty Dumpty is on page 19

The cow who jumped over the moon is on page 17

Ba Ba Black Sheep is on page 5

Nanny Goat appears on pages 9, 17, 20

Published by b small publishing, Pinewood, 3a Coombe Ridings, Kingston upon Thames, Surrey KT2 7JT
© b small publishing, 1998
1 2 3 4 5

Colour reproduction: Vimnice International Ltd., Hong Kong.   Printed in Hong Kong by Wing King Tong Co. Ltd.
Design: Lone Morton   *Editorial:* Marta Fumagalli and Catherine Bruzzone   *Production:* Grahame Griffiths
ISBN 1 874735 29 8
British Library Cataloguing-in-Publication Data. A catalogue record for this book is available from the British Library.